BLOSSOM THOUGHTS

POEMS OF HOPE, INSPIRATION, BELIEF, LOVE AND DETERMINATION

BY

HEMLATA PORALKAR

Isbn 123456789012345
© Hemlata Poralkar 2020
Published In India 2020 By Pencil

A Brand Of
One Point Six Technologies Pvt. Ltd.
123, Building J2, Shram Seva Premises,
Wadala Truck Terminal, Wadala (E)
Mumbai 400037, Maharashtra, India
E Connect@Thepencilapp.Com
W Www.Thepencilapp.Com

DISCLAIMER: *The opinions expressed in this book are those of the authors and do not purport to reflect the views of the Publisher.*

Author biography

BLOSSOM THOUGHTS

Hemlata Poralkar, a Science graduate student and her love for books started at childhood makes her voracious creative in a sense and diversifed vision. She describes herself by penning own quote- " *I am a kind of bunch of flower, who loves diversity of fragrance always.* " She loves art, reading, writing, painting, playing, singing, talking, nature, travelling specially historical places and trekking.

She believes that we should try all the things and don't say 'It is not belongs to me further love it, do it and see it." Her confidence and self-believeness is like a third eye to tackle a failure.

With higher education her passion for reading and writing always in a pocket. Though being a Science student she has interest agogly in a History and Polity to connect with humanity.

She writes in a fiction manner but closely related with human society. Marathi, English and Hindi is a language for her to write.

She has participated in many Poetry Competitions and writes for many platforms like Storymirror, YourQuote, Pratilipi etc.

She has written in a Marathi Magazine also.

Contents

On New Year Eve

Note To Reader

Epigraph

<u>BLOSSOM THOUGHTS</u> (Poems of Hope, Inspiration, Belief, Love and Determination)

'Poetry is a life changing platform if one can understand it fully'

Hemlata Poralkar

Preface

I am so greatful today that all intuition makes me so strong for writing poetry in deep manner.

Dedicate these all poems to reader, I thought these will be giving ray of hope, love, determination, fearless soul and courage.

I believe words have a power that would change one's life thoroughly. My love for writing and reading is blessings for me to write by heart and being my own support system in every situation of life.

I am going to start this book with my poem ' Alive Poetry' in a sense of what's the mean of poem in life.

I thank to all my well-wishers and closest one to help me in a random manner.

The way I found a ray in these poem I hope it will spread to the one's. I give my best till my last tunnel.

For my readers, for your love and support.

This one's for you.

Acknowledgements

My parents and sisters blessings for their help in making this book and gone through it lovingly.

Specially, Pencil platform who gives enthusiastic opportunity to showcase my writing skill as per need.

A Song From The Suds

Queen of my tub, I merrily sing,
While the white foam raises high,
And sturdily wash, and rinse, and wring,
And fasten the clothes to dry;
Then out in the free fresh air they swing,
Under the sunny sky.

I wish we could wash from our hearts and our souls
The stains of the week away,
And let water and air by their magic make
Ourselves as pure as they;
Then on the earth there would be indeed
A glorious washing day!

Along the path of a useful life
Will heart's-ease ever bloom;
The busy mind has no time to think
Of sorrow, or care, or gloom;
And anxious thoughts may be swept away
As we busily wield a broom.

I am glad a task to me is given
To labor at day by day;
For it brings me health, and strength, and hope,
And I cheerfully learn to say-

'Head, you may think; heart, you may feel;
But hand, you shall work always!'

-By Louisa May Alcott.

Alive Poetry

(The poem tells about what a means of poetry in our life.
Eternal alive we are by poetry itself*.)*

As I start to write
My heart and mind closely tight,
Only words run as fast as
On paddle tract with unknown miles.

Melodies of birds
Wind blows with touching archly
Surreptitiously it does
Just pouring in my eyes.

Agony feels on face scar
But poetry fill deep that,
Only scarlet like empathy knows it
Keenly I get that.

Inspire dwells here
Source of happiness mingle,
I can see deep in the ocean
I can feel rise of dawn.

Life is, a scribe poetry

Own has their own pen;
Not like to call poet always; only in a sense
We alive; poetry live and we alive again,
Though healing slowly but poetry alive again!

I Am Woman With...

**(Woman, one word with full of meaning.
Here I portray shades of woman on her own canvas.)**

As colorful as none other
In a picturesque canvas than
My attitude has
Butterfly hues together.

I have a grief but
Don't extend it beyond my happy line;
It is deeply fine in my heart
It is rhythm of mine breathe.

Yes, uncountable scars I got
Trapped in unexpectable spot,
Willingly, a fire of fight still blows now
Gives courage myself to glow.

Tranquil, I feel it is like my child
Neither can relief from something than
Adoring with beloved child
Curiously, I find my own way
Even in a bleakest blind.

I fetch from my undry well

A livingly gratitude,
Sometimes I found in full of apathy
Due to circumstances therapy;
Still, I have a warmth
Indigenously born.

I am woman with...
Changeable frequency voice
Possession of integrity character;
I have a passion with compassion
For my alive screenplay
As being real kind always!

So, I am woman with...
Owner of my own bliss bank!

We Are All Born...

(There is a purpose of everything in a nature. Be a part of it, we born as a gift. So, for what we have here is like an uncover our life mystery.
Born to know, know for grow *.)*

We are all born for what...?
As an angel for our parents, absolutely it is
But is that enough?

We are all born for what...?
As a buddy for siblings and colleagues, exactly it is
But is that enough?

We are all born for what...?
Making bond of relationship with someone, surely it is
But is that enough?

It's a heap of ups and downs
It's an ocean of emotions
Naturally, life of a born infant it is

But is that enough?

Let's then reload the journey of life
Start to explore a word 'enough' more bright,

Destiny will say, "Come on, Triumph, takes flight."

We are all born...
To see a horizon of our belief morn,
What are you; makes day happy as you want,
Banish all limit and light up in a dark
Born day should like a new flower blossom in a park.

We are all born...beyond 'enough' at all...

A Dreaming Dreamer

(Dream is like a wish tree and we feel, it will be happened
in a reality as well. But there is difference between dream
and reality
as like a day and night.
However, one can not forget about our presence between
this. This presence gives us strength to deal with both and
become a dreaming dreamer always.)

When I was in a midnight, subconciously tight
A miracle came across me and I stuck into it,
Like a splendor statue;
I wanted ought to there, shall all have in a mine fist.

Unwillingly, sun rays touches me to awake
Brings me in a conscious dream,
Eyes so big, a body is going to straight,
What has happened, just contemplating in any way.

It is visual, not a virtual world
Not shall all come as easy as,
I must strive for my ambition
I must redefine myself.

To achieve that fruitful, try to boost more ways
As like the sun does by liberating lightning rays.

I was a night dreamer so far
Now, might be a day dreamer; but not an alone
Night and day, both have in a hopeful manner
Only being as a dreaming dreamer
A dreaming dreamer...

Like

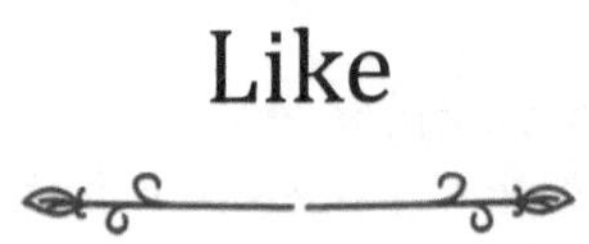

(Like, I want to be like something, not for, I feel inferior but
stretch myself to reach superiority. I believe all power rest
in our own but
we enclose it inferiorly.
So, enjoy our life and try to be 'like' to mould ownself
not for other's sake.)

Not too much, not too little
Just smile like I make it,
Jump over and over
Perhaps I can touch to height.

Beautified faces see again and again
Mirror has to obey my rule anyway,
Say,"I see myself queen always."

Like a breeze can sway
Like a storm held a rage,
Some lie with truth mash
It is 'Okay' life with both have.

Like a rose with thorn made
Warmth face and soul shine in heart ease all a same.

I like to see my shadow

It can be my love,care and true penny,
Also fight for those eyes
Who limits my felicity quite.

I am constantly sharpening my way
By hard work ethic axe,
Triumph or fall; It is all hell
Pocket of struggle meant to get
Okay! Okay! sound of mine tell.

I like to be strong, more strong
Gravity holds me once fell down,
If alone, I will find my inner trench
Or, If I found in a crowd then will reach to that human self;
Know the world and watering full of grace!

I like be like whatsoever here
Cause I have felt my tale in every image well
Now, I am waiting for new 'like' I will be
Till last door of dwell !

Tears In An Eyes

(Tear, drop by drop, sometimes like running flow. Don't take it as trouble but wear it as our healing cream.
Tear can never make difference between man and woman.
It dwells into eyes of every creature of nature.
Nerves of thoughts are closely connect with tears and generate impluse of strongest ever .)

Those twinkling stars
By refracting light,
But our eyes droplet
Glittering by someone more bright.

Tear is an ideal forever
Would be from grief,
Could be from bliss,
We wear as it is, however.

No need to wipe out
It's a thoughts of running,
It will be strength one day
Path is soon clearing.

Tears, Tears, Tears
You feel truly dear,

You have in our eyes
We can see even in a blind.

~ 23 ~

Fly Above The Sky

*(This is a loop form of poetry type. There are no restrictions
on the number of stanzas nor on the syllable counts
for each line.
In each stanza, the last word of the first line becomes
the first word of second line.
In this poem, more focus is given to positive vision of human
being.* **Stay positive to take high jump and
lead life till brave blood flows in a body.)**

I would be happy
Happy to take fly
Fly with wings of courage
Courage can never die.

Blindful storms frontly face
Face with strongful hand
Hand in hand puts step
Step turns in dream land.

Mind box is full of stuff
Stuff of blissful thoughts
Thoughts can push up
Up always where we want.

Sooner to take jump high
High can never stop
Stop turns wind can
Can I fly above the sky?
Sky sures heroism is in one's hand.

Learning For Change

(Learning should be first from inward and tend to move
outword globally for change.
What would we like to learn, grasp it passionately and
change our surrounding ethically.)

A task we have taken
The matters all here,
Tackle it; confront it
Some left hand in hand will be there.

Our body is working
Mind acts as an engine,
Strenuously one heart
Companionly accelerating.

We have a passion
Don't know, where it comes from?
We like to do best
I think innards want.

It's a learning path
Whatever we shall do;
For what we are here so,
Nothing is in mine

Only present can predict though,
We must learn and learn
For changing within
To moulding view
By dauntless glue.

Thoughts

(Thought is a part of life . We can not live a single moment without it. In whatever sense it is but will be there always.)

Can I see it ?
Only my brain box is juggling with it,
Can I feel it?
Only my heartbeat is tunning with it.

Can I speak with it?
When my word tunes into mirror image with it,
Can I play with it?
When I am proudly stand with it.

Can I sleep with it?
Yes, when my dream wants sword like it,
Can I eat with it?
Surely, thoughts have taste of opinion with.

Can I make it as my routine?
I am just gonna say it is silly to ask,
Can I live without it?
It will never be happen at all.

Transparency Like A Water

(Transparency is a value added word in life if,
one can use it properly.
**Water taught me the importance of transperancy in
life.**

**A penetration of rays [that rays might be of success or
failure in our life] needs transparent water to reach
into deep
then ecosytem survive.
Like this we should be transparent so that rays can
penetrate and reach to thc goal.)**

*As I thought with my growing sense
My eyes is my vision,
Through I have seen
Beautiful blue diamond.*

*Glittering in my mind more
Than reflecting by an eyes,
Dipping down and touches a floor
Is a water mystery
Missed in a deep core.*

Light of shining rays

Travelling above my head,
Reached the water surface
Like destiny gets their bed.

Stuck in a mind
How does a lightning rays penetrate it?
Smooth surface of water it is
How does ray pass through it?

Drops of water jumped over me
Said is a quality of mine,
Still with effluent and slurry quite
Transparency ours last sign.

How much darkness behind;
Transparency must be for penetration of light!

Now, I get the mean
For my destination of life
Finger print must be crystal clear in a rife.

Whatever Struggle face
Don't try to change in any case,
Rays find their path soon
Transparency is like boon.

Imperfection Is A Perfection

(Imperfection is a strength for giving our best.
Not for anyone but for me I want to be always
on a path of improving.
For this my 'Imperfections' is a sword to lead a life
in a random manner.)

*As I child, didn't know
What a word is this "Miss Perfect",
But my mother knew it very well
Makeover she tried but something was neglect.*

*My baby should be like
Stars can feel inferior even be,
Ruby like chick; dressed shine in a diamond feel
Crown of clusters and stand up with a colourful heel.
Mother wants this for her child's happiness
But being perfect is not last door.*

*Fantasy of life is going with perfect
In friendship, relationship even in
A dream career and in old age garden
We strive for it restlessly;
Get then depress innard
With more deform outword.*

Consequences of perfection
Will find in a fear for imperfection,
Then mistake and failure
Feels life full of disgrace.

Not at all it is weakness
Lead our life; is a clearness
I am an imperfect say with a greatness.

Improve is a mirror image
Imperfect is a way
Not for others to be perfect
But from within I must say.

A Burning Candle

**(A burning candle tells us we can help someone
who are fighting with their darken days.
It is a gratitude for us to do for someone without
expect anything.)**

*As I sat in a obscure darkness
I had nothing to see
Got into mind blockness;
Slowly darken turned to brighten
Could only done by
Ambitious burning candle.*

*Glimpsely I could see
Path was ready to take
Just contemplating with my brain
How was this single candle enough to make?*

*I curiously wanted to know
Candle started to disclose,
"It is not a bizarre things
It is hidden mystery of human beings."*

*Candle urgely said-
"I have inborn ability to burn*

Light up with shiny rays;
To kill a darken trap
As a source for other
By painful dwindling myself."

For someone it is
My reciprocally gratitude!
To do for happiness
Nothing like to expect
Such a piece of priceless.

I keenly get that
Be a burning candle for someone
Not only for beloved one's
My eyes also on stranger,
I will burn for them
To see behind darken
More brighten days,
I can help generously
As a burning candle
Fortitudinously...

Thank You Teacher

**(Teacher is an universal creature for learning.
I have shown here a teacher in our three phase of life
i.e. child age, adult age and old age differently.)**

*In a three phase of life
We can't live without you,
In a sparkle fountain garden
Our childhood, adulthood and old age blossom.*

*In a three phase of life
First single finger touches by our heart,
Parents are the first role model
We are twinkling stars of their eye!*

*We can see a glory, they help us to feel it
We can fight by hand, they make strong bonny,
We can speak with limit, they tell start to explore
Such a 'Childhood Basket' full of honey.*

*In a three phase of life
Move towards adulty and a whole hand tightly hold,
This is a time to jump in a circus
Different faces of people can see in a fold.*

More experiences, more recognitions

More rejections still hope full leader,
But on a way, I am not one
Front and behind races ladder.

In a three phase of life
Old age is a new age,
The body is going to fragile
Still, the flower of lesson pour over a child.

In a three phase of life
Meet all that unseen teacher,
Some in school or unknown somewhere
Blessed we have and ready to say-
"Thank you, Teacher" for being in my three phase
forever.

Rain All Over

(I wrote this poem in Pune city.
In 2019, there was flooded rain all over city.
We want rainwater in specific quantity but if it crosses limit
then
drastic effect seen into environment.
Here, I request rain to clear soon.)

What a heavy rain!
What a heavy rain!
Why doesn't it want to stop now then?

Such a bombarding shower
Overflow buckets here and there,
Once eye gets so wet
Hidden sorrow never anyone can guess.

Soothing can feel
A droplets of diamond,
I rejoice it much more like
But now want a limit bond.

Clouds are so dark
Fill as unwanted bazaar,
Hurridely wants to discharge
Again become clear so far.

People of water planet
Playing hide and seek with sunshine,
But never catch ever now

Eye sticks to sky of mine.

Sun strives for free so hard
But dirty cloud stands as a wall,
What a miracle this is!
Life struggle this is call.

Oh! Rain...!Oh! Rain...!
Thirsty throat is wet away,
Such a bissful you are
Let's help for come back again
Only want routine day.

For Our Motherland

(For our motherland...Our Bharat ...Our Pride...,this poem
I have written for our javan who fight for us tirelessly.
We don't know what is going over battlefield just feel and
see
how it will be fine soon.
So, this poem salutes to my javan brother for their great
work .)

*Whole my body at home
But my brainy box with beating heart
Is on a border gone.*

*I don't know what's going there
Still I am suspect here
My 'Javan' brothers fight so hard
Motherland shadow shades all
Telling me for your well
They stand on border as their dwell.*

*I knew war yet not see at all
I knew stories but assume it all,
Such a bloody grassland
Feel a pride; they fight hard for victor,
Unfortunately, I am here
Just praying mere.*

I live in a peace
Their gift for me,
Heroes of thousand eyes
Ready to fight for we,
It's time to look for change
From motherland to battlefield.

See with glimpse
I soulfully feel,
How they confront
Opponent fire in a deal,
What a strength for their
Our 'TIRANGA' foremost prime here.

Flag of valour stand courageously
When 'JAVAN' is holding
I admit myself patriotic as being.

Live for nation, live with passion
Fraternity bond makes stronger
For our motherland
Till last forever.

Unknown

**(Unknown somewhere for sometimes it is best to feel
free and no need to think about anything.
I think we must choose it for once.)**

*I gonna want to be
Unknown somewhere
And I am the one
With wind blows along me there.*

*Never ever want to
Juggling with thoughts and
Hammering for understand,
I just want to magically disappear.*

*Don't like to find anything else
Now eye blinks so less,
I try to read a book
But words are hidden in a page.*

*Things might be know
Seat along with me side place,
I will ignore it unknownly
It is fine in some case.*

I seek for that place

Where blankly unknown feel,
Birds will be chirping with me
And known can heal.

Through The Window Side

(Window, it is place where we feel our life.
Happiness, sadness, anger, hope and love
can see through window side.
So, through the window side life is born and die .)

I stand on side and day by day across
Night knew my look, witness of dots

Brick brown color wall, tangle bougainvillea all
What I thought, messed up and flushed scars.

Gentleman came for round then saw me like statue
And I waited for wind, my silence mixes as high as need jet
stream.

Bird chirped a word, fluttering loudly wings
I filled with tears, eyes bulged with things.

When heart dress up delights, rustle leaves welcome of
mine
I will sing a song, dance in melodies vine.

Some vein flows in anger, cloud converts in darken
Lightning so strong, rain stops the fire.

I dream through the window side
My birth inside and death outside
I feel presence in sqaure window tight.

This Too Shall Pass

(If we believe we have hope then will find a way. This is core
of poem.
In 2020, Corona Pandemic around the world
and how people are facing it with the hope
is depict from the poem.)

All over here, in the world of despair
Only hope with unity in pair.

People mind is in turmoil
Catch up in a cage,
What to do? What should we do?
Such a stuff of narrow edge.

Put up mask on mouth
Only eyes so big to know,
Whole body is paralysed
In quarantine home.

Chalk and duster schools
Grassy playground mood,
Such a gusto moment
Has missed by crowd.

Rules now in a square box

Ways to say for never cross,
Now, understand the 'Survival Of Fittest'
Take a bitter along sweet toss.

No one is left now
Ready to deal in mettle,
How warrior life is!
No stone is unturned to settle.

Resilient strong we are
Face it till fell down,
Belongs to valour realm
Let's all stand up and say-
" This too shall pass, sooner all."

A Magic Of Three Pearl

(It is a piece of prose-poem form. Imagination, symbols, emotions and metaphor are used here in a deep. The poem looks like in a narrative sense and Anne is a lead character. A word magic brings unexpected things. But from this poem, Anne, needs that magic for begin new one and change her life. It means sometimes we would like some magic to happen in our life and change our ups and downs.)

At a midnight light, Anne, opened her eyes, star bright the night,
wind blew in hide and sea waves jumped silently on large stone.

It was surprise to see, she stood with big eyes and put steps heavily.

Her footsteps mixed with sand, patches could see behind, sea waves called her, eyes became glisten dark.

She went close and water hugged eagerly, in a moment, three pearl saw and waves left place quickly.

Anne wonder, what was that?
Pearl magic discovery has been started.

Pearl shell was happy to see, opened in speed and pearls
jumped over Anne.

One pearl magically stuck on neck and bloomed in
beautiful necklace,
other found over finger and shining ring made.

Last pearl missed on sea bed, Anne was again amazed,
later she left a place in a fearfull face,
along with her one pearl followed steps.

She reached home, face frightened show,
she laid on bed, body enclosed in a roll.

All night was passed, sun rises high, a new day start
Anne has three pearl now magic begins for new land.

Chapati

Chapati, is a history of struggle since years till now. Chapati can make difference between poor and rich. Here, I want to tell how Chapati is more important than life in each ones.)

A delicious plate
Decorate well,
Chapati *is a king*
For conquer and protect.

It is made up of wheat flour
Flourish by different names,
Taste of hand mixes
Love in brown puff,
Origin in our subcontinent.

Rolled by Belan
And thrown on heated Tava ,
Chapati is a staple for
Learn more and more.

Measure diameter
Of Roti,
Person to person,
Some gets more
Some losses in a hope,

Is a struggle ground
Since years till now.

Sleep Well

*(It is a lullaby, usually the mother, sings to her child
to make it go to sleep well.She makes her child sleep
beautiful by lovely things.)*

*From my eyes
I send a dream,
You find the land
I give the key.*

*You can see
The magic world
And fly with wings,
If fear you feel
I give hand in hand your.*

*I sing a song
You enjoy in a dimple smile,
I put hand
Over forehead
With soft care,
Will say-
Sleep well.*

Bookmark

(Each and every aspect of life is important and
I want to preserve it by bookmark.
Bookmark for where we are.)

I encircle all the ways
Chocolates of delight
And sorrow full pain,
I see the light
Of win and fail,
I find in a room
Deep feel and love,
One slice of friends
And other of my love
I hide some and seek for life,
I have not much in hand
But not even empty,
I save all this
And highlight in a dark colour,
When I miss it
Bookmark goes in a search.

I Find The Key Of Treasure

(Treasure is a hope for us. From this poem, a girl search for the key
of her treasure and inside it what she wants in life like
happiness, hope, inspiration, love, care, win, etc., is closed. But
she tensed because could not find the key. Lastly, Poetess
assures from the side of a girl that the key of treasure is
within yourself.
What we search is inside you and have to explore.)

Whole the room
I searched till night,
Tired and restlessed
On the bed I laid down,
I sought inside the *Almari*
and peeped into the cupboard,
All things spread on floor
I puzzled and tensed,
Door silently closed
I was hidden these from other.

A treasure
I saw at night,
It was full of gifts
what I want in life

It was still inside,
Made up of wood
And glass lid over,
Lock sign could see
Just glass key was missed,
I wake up at dawn
And eagerly look around.

Lastly, I find the key of treasure
Within mine.

How Can I Left It

(It is some what like sonnet as a lyrical of fourteen lines.
Theme of the poem is love between a girl and her father.
But due to certain circumstances she could not believe
on her father for what he had done with her family.
She is addressing what her father image in her eyes.
Now, she is in dilemma would she hate or believe.)

Shall I hate you from my deepest part
Memories behind, bright full tight,
I can, do peculiar, you said obstinate smart
Make thoughts strong cross all plight,
And you paid love in priceless stock
Sometimes heaven knocked next door,
Season came and gone; you handled my clock
Whatever can happen even fortune taste sour,
Shaped me and said mountain makes history
Then how I think like, edge weep loud,
Your fair fond looks trouble mistry
But foregone love will afresh cloud
Should I hate or not, yet fate desire
Still garden fragrance spread from your attire

I Made A Tale At Child

(A poem tells us how poetess made stories in childhood and told her friends. At a childhood, we don't know how to tell a tale but we did it in full confidence but was a part of fun we enjoyed a lot.)

I didn't know
How to assemble,
I knew a tiger and lion
It looked funny said.

Character I had taken from
Whatever I saw,
I thought in a deep
Eyes on searched path.

I stole words
Each one from all,
Moral of the story
Was so far and far.

It was happy childish
To made tale for tell,
Compete with others
Was not the aim,

Everyone won the prize
Of laughter,
And end the game.

I Save The Coins

*(From childhood we know how to collect money and
in adulthood we understand it's importance to save it.)*

*I had a piggy bank
Made up of pottery,
I saved more Chillar
For chocolates and toys,
Sometimes stole from pockets
And said I won reward,
Parents knew very well
Secretly I hid all,
On one stage forward
I had a pocket money
Like home governance
Monthly scholarship,
Next with this
Added school admission bonus
Now officially bank holder,
Grown up further
Saved and collected happily coins.
It's time to multiple
By own hand,*

And difficult to do
Seriously hard,
I save the coins now
Feel satisfy.

I Learn From You

*(It is romance poem. A poetess finds a love difference between
her and beloved one. She likes the way of his loving
and wants to learn love from his eyes.)*

I count a stars
You look on moon,
I hide a words
You spell in a loud,
I like a bed of lilies
You water more for life,
I dress up beautiful colors
For you love is attire,
I lost a one day
You add in the next day,
I love to see nature
You feel in care,
You love in a deep
I learn from you.

Bookshelf

A poetess describes her bookshelf in a decorative manner.
A bookshelf is like her family member.
Lastly, she wants her own books in her bookshelf
hopefully.)

*I talk with you
From early day,
I choose you
Foremost jewel,
When I search for new
Words are fight with each other,
I pick up one
Others show displeasure,
I arrange in order
From A to Z,
Start with aim
To destiny end game,
Decorate well
Book cover tells,
Dust can spread
Reveal how much history spent,
I dance in rhythm
Poet recites their spell,
I perform the character
Novel gives me*

In any page,
I wonder in a histories
Autobiographies motivate
And wait for horror
Suspense also bell,
I romance in a way
Like Shakespeare sonnet,
I want to flick the wand
From Harry Potter series wizard
Like Hermione said "Wingardium Leviosa",
I have some education base
Collect and save more knowledge
In a understaning gets,
I dream for new one
Every aspects of land
Begins from India
To the world around,
Then vision of my eye
Write more and more
And I pen down my own
Bookshelf welcome in a row.

Think Deep

*(A multitasking habbit connects more neuron and sharpen
the personality which makes life happy.)*

She was sitting on a stair
Busy with work,
Writing in one hand
Painting brush on the other,
Eyes upon the books
Mind goes in multi-tasking look.

I wonder how she could
We sometimes don't want to do,
Barriers we create
And left it soon,
I wanted to know
Then joined her company,
She would reveal the secret
And I was there to steal.

She believes
That we are born to multiply,
Think deep and superior
Feel you are,

What you do
Passion creates all.

Places I Want To Travel

*(From this poem, a poetess tells us how will she explore
her travelling in a broad ways. She has only seen places in a
books
and learn about it but now she wants to go out and feel it.)*

From Top to bottom
And East to West,
I want to travel
Explore my lens.

A places I will visit
Mountains,Rivers as companion
All journey path,
Different regions cross
Knows about ethnic diversity form,
A stories of kings
I will hear from petrichor,
How the battle was fought?
I will listen from indigeneous people,
Their rules and regulations
Culture and lifestyle
I will read from the
Art and architecture,
I will taste food

And note down one by one
Cuisines would teach new traditions,
What I learned from book
I want to see frontly
And passion of travelling
Help to reach.

Love Through A Letter

*(A poem is wriiten in a letter format by poetess to her love.
She send a love through letter in a romantic way.)*

Dear Love,

I write a letter
To send you love,

I failed to tell

And fainted below.

How much you love
I unable to measure,
I feel the night
And write up
In an ambience.

I spread the words
Like flowers garden
I send my love
In a fresh fragrance,
I use colourful pens
Cause found you
In different shade,
And each word mirror image

Of your love made,
I give strong full stop
For unique I thought,
Each lines pen down
Theme of your fond,
Care, trust and friendship
I mean it's strong,
And you deserve
Get till last,
Each paragraph
Like layers of cream
I gift you cake
Letter for love.

Your Love.

On New Year Eve

**(A New Year Eve Day is a hopeful day and
celebrates for coming new year.
Poetess describes how she celebrates and give
motivating message for new year in the last lines of the
poem.)**

*I am excited
To celebrate
A new year eve
Let go all behind
Welcome new morn.*

*I decorate a desk
With pestries and chocolates
Gather the happiness
And send wishes in a card.*

*I invite all beloved
Precious gifts I serve
A bell rings in a loud
Make resolutions in a prayer.*

*I decide to announce
A message by heart
"We are born*

For new born
A new year gives a chance."

Note To Reader

Dear Readers ,

This book is base on fiction but reality flows from it. **Poetry, is a running thoughts, gives edge to life.** Poems of hope, determination, self- believeness, love, learning, fearlessness, etc., is a gift for us and from my side I wrapped it in my thoughts to reach quickly to your heart and mind.

The message that I also wanted to convey through this poetry book is that never feel inferior and do what you like and share by your words.

My aim to write this book is to connect my thoughts with you and want to learn more from you after reading this once.

I thank you to all my readers and your suggestions will help me to write more better.

I have mentioned a poem " **A Songs From The Suds** " by **Louisa May Alcott** is a playful teen poem. In this poem poetess relates philosophy of life by her work **washing**

cloth and last lines of this poem so inspiring and tell us must be busy with our work happily.

"How can one poem change our life by words!" I think is a gift.

If you have been inspired quite by this book and if you have enjoyed it, I would consider my task is complete.

"World is full of words and we born to grasp it."

Hemlata Poralkar

Notes

For reader's view-

After reading all this poems, I feel you can confidently express your views and admire it.

So, for what you are waiting, let's ready to pen down soon...